Buddy's Summer Day

The Sound of Short U

by Cecilia Minden and Joanne Meier • illustrated by Bob Ostrom

The Child's World

Published by The Child's World®
1980 Lookout Drive
Mankato, MN 56003-1705
800-599-READ
www.childsworld.com

The Child's World®: Mary Berendes, Publishing Director
The Design Lab: Design and page production

Library of Congress Cataloging-in-Publication Data
Minden, Cecilia.
  Buddy's summer day : the sound of short U / by Cecilia
Minden and Joanne Meier ; illustrated by Bob Ostrom.
    p. cm.
  ISBN 978-1-60253-418-6 (library bound : alk. paper)
  1. English language—Vowels—Juvenile literature.
  2. English language—Phonetics—Juvenile literature.
  3. Reading—Phonetic method—Juvenile literature. I. Meier,
Joanne D. II. Ostrom, Bob. III. Title.
  PE1157.M5635 2010
  [E]—dc22   2010005614

Printed in the United States of America in Mankato, MN.
July 2010
F11538

NOTE TO PARENTS AND EDUCATORS:

The Child's World® has created this series with the goal of exposing children to engaging stories and illustrations that assist in phonics development. The books in the series will help children learn the relationships between the letters of written language and the individual sounds of spoken language. This contact helps children learn to use these relationships to read and write words.

The books in this series follow a similar format. An introductory page, to be read by an adult, introduces the child to the phonics feature, or sound, that will be highlighted in the book. Read this page to the child, stressing the phonic feature. Help the student learn how to form the sound with her mouth. The story and engaging illustrations follow the introduction. At the end of the story, word lists categorize the feature words into their phonic elements.

Each book in this series has been carefully written to meet specific readability requirements. Close attention has been paid to elements such as word count, sentence length, and vocabulary. Readability formulas measure the ease with which the text can be read and understood. Each book in this series has been analyzed using the Spache readability formula.

Reading research suggests that systematic phonics instruction can greatly improve students' word recognition, spelling, and comprehension skills. This series assists in the teaching of phonics by providing students with important opportunities to apply their knowledge of phonics as they read words, sentences, and text.

The letter u makes two sounds.

The long sound of **u** sounds like **u** as in: *cute* and *tube*.

The short sound of **u** sounds like **u** as in: *mud* and *up*.

In this book, you will read words that have the short **u** sound as in: *bugs, ducks, run,* and *mud*.

Buddy is happy.

It is a bright summer day.

There is so much to do!

Buddy likes to hunt for bugs. Some bugs are as small as buttons. Some bugs hum when they fly.

Buddy feeds the ducks from a cup.

A duck jumps to get the food. He must be very hungry!

Buddy likes to run.

His puppy, Tuffy, runs too.

Tuffy runs in the mud.

Now his fur is full of mud.

"Oh, Tuffy, you look funny!" says Buddy.
"I'll get the mud off you."

Buddy brushes Tuffy.

He rubs off the mud.

It is time for supper.
We're having bread
and butter. Yummy!

Fun Facts

Did you know that people have recorded eating 462 different types of bugs? Someone even came up with a recipe for "chocolate chirpie cookies"—a special treat that contains chocolate chips, chopped nuts, and crickets! But be sure and talk to your parents before you get hungry and head for your backyard.
Not all bugs are safe to eat, and even the ones that are usually need to be prepared a certain way.

Do you like the warm weather in summer? When the weather is chilly in winter, remember that people who live south of the *equator* are enjoying their summer. The equator is an imaginary line that runs around the middle of Earth at a halfway point between the North and South poles. During our winter months, Earth turns in a way that makes the sun closer to people who live south of the equator.

Activity

Keeping a Bug House
Visit your local library to learn about keeping a bug house. You can either buy a ready-made bug house or use household items such as old jam or pickle jars with holes punched in the lids. Check to make sure that the bugs you plan to keep will get along with each other. Find out what each bug will need to eat. Consider releasing the bugs back into the wild after you have studied them for a few days.

To Learn More

Books
About the Sound of Short U
Moncure, Jane Belk. *My "u" Sound Box®*. Mankato, MN: The Child's World, 2009.

About Bugs
Rompella, Natalie. *Don't Squash That Bug!: The Curious Kid's Guide to Insects*. Montréal: Lobster Press, 2007.
Shields, Carol Diggory, and Scott Nash (illustrator). *The Bugliest Bug*. Cambridge, MA: Candlewick Press, 2002.

About Mud
Anderson, Jean. *Amazing Mud*. Logan, IA: Perfection Learning, 2006.
Ray, Mary Lyn, and Lauren Stringer (illustrator). *Mud*. San Diego: Harcourt Inc., 2001.

About Summer
Low, Alice, and Roy McKie (illustrator). *Summer*. New York: Beginner Books, 1991.
Pickering, Jimmy. *It's Summer*. Los Angeles: Smallfellow Press, 2003.

Web Sites
Visit our home page for lots of links about the Sound of Short U:
childsworld.com/links

Note to Parents, Teachers, and Librarians: We routinely check our Web links to make sure they're safe, active sites—so encourage your readers to check them out!

Short U
Feature Words

Proper Names
Buddy   Tuffy

Feature Words in Medial Position

bug	jump
butter	much
button	mud
cup	must
duck	puppy
full	rub
funny	run
hum	summer
hungry	supper
hunt	yummy

Feature Word with Blends
brush

About the Authors

Cecilia Minden, PhD, is the former director of the Language and Literacy Program at the Harvard Graduate School of Education. She is now a reading consultant for school and library publications. She earned her PhD in reading education from the University of Virginia. Cecilia and her husband, Dave Cupp, live outside Chapel Hill, North Carolina. They enjoy sharing their love of reading with their grandchildren, Chelsea and Qadir.

Joanne Meier, PhD, has worked as an elementary school teacher, university professor, and researcher. She earned her BA in early childhood education from the University of South Carolina, and her MEd and PhD in education from the University of Virginia. She currently works as a literacy consultant for schools and private organizations. Joanne lives in Virginia with her husband Eric, daughters Kella and Erin, two cats, and a gerbil.

About the Illustrator

Bob Ostrom has been illustrating children's books for nearly twenty years. A graduate of the New England School of Art & Design at Suffolk University, Bob has worked for such companies as Disney, Nickelodeon, and Cartoon Network. He lives in North Carolina with his wife Melissa and three children, Will, Charlie, and Mae.